William Julius Mickle

Almada Hill

An Epistle from Lisbon

William Julius Mickle

Almada Hill
An Epistle from Lisbon

ISBN/EAN: 9783337327279

Printed in Europe, USA, Canada, Australia, Japan

Cover: Foto ©Andreas Hilbeck / pixelio.de

More available books at **www.hansebooks.com**

ALMADA HILL:

A N

EPISTLE

FROM

LISBON.

By *WILLIAM JULIUS MICKLE.*

OXFORD,
PRINTED BY W. JACKSON:
And fold by J. Bew, Paternofter-Row, London; and by the Bookfellers of Oxford and Cambridge.

MDCCLXXXI.

ADVERTISEMENT.

THOUGH no subjects are more proper for poetry than those which are founded upon historical retrospect, the author of such a poem lies under very particular disadvantages: every one can understand and relish a work merely fictitious, descriptive, or sentimental; but a previous acquaintance, and even intimacy, with the history and characters upon which the other poem is founded, is absolutely necessary to do justice to its author. Without such previous knowledge, the ideas which he would convey pass unobserved, as in an unknown tongue; and the happiest allusion, if he is fortunate enough to attain any thing worthy of that name, is unfelt and unseen. Under these disadvantages the following epistle is presented to the public, whose indulgence and candour the author has already amply experienced.

In the Twelfth Century, Lisbon, and great part of Portugal and Spain, were in possession of the Moors. Alphonso, the first King of Portugal, having gained several victories over that people, was laying fiege to Lifbon, when Robert, Duke of Gloucefter, on his way to the Holy Land, appeared upon the coaft of that kingdom. As the caufe was the fame, Robert was eafily perfuaded to make his firft crufade in Portugal. He demanded that the ftorming of the Caftle of Lifbon, fituated on a confiderable hill, and whofe ruins fhew it to have been of great ftrength, fhould be allotted to him, while Alphonfo was to affail the walls and the city. Both Leaders were fuccefsful; and Alphonfo, among the rewards which he beftowed upon the Englifh, granted to thofe who were wounded, or unable to proceed to Paleftine, the Caftle of Almada, and the adjoining lands.

The river Tagus below and oppofite to Lifbon, is edged by fteep grotefque rocks, particularly on the fouth fide. Thofe on the fouth are generally higher and much more magnificent and picturefque than the Cliffs of Dover. Upon one of the higheft of thefe, and directly oppofite to Lifbon, remain the ftately ruins of the Caftle of Almada.

In December, 1779, as the Author was wandering among thefe ruins, he was ftruck with the idea, and formed the plan of the following poem; an idea which, it may be allowed

allowed, was natural to the Tranflator of the LUSIAD, and the plan may, in fome degree, be called a fupplement to that work.

The following poem, except the corrections and a few lines, was written in Portugal. The defcriptive parts are ftrictly local. The fineft profpect of Lifbon and the Tagus, (which is there about four miles broad) is from Almada, which alfo commands the adjacent country, from the Rock of Cintra to the Caftle and City of Palmela, an extent of above fifty miles. This magnificent view is completed by the extenfive opening at the mouth of the Tagus, about ten miles below, which difcovers the Atlantic Ocean.

A N

E P I S T L E

F R O M

L I S B O N.

―――――――

WHILE you, my Friend, from louring wintery plains
    Now pale with fnows, now black with drizzling rains,
From leaflefs woodlands, and difhonour'd bowers
Mantled by gloomy mifts, or lafh'd by fhowers
Of hollow moan, while not a ftruggling beam
Steals from the Sun to play on Ifis' ftream;
While from thefe fcenes by England's winter fpread
Swift to the cheerful hearth your fteps are led,
Pleas'd from the threatening tempeft to retire
And join the circle round the focial fire;

B.   In

In other clime through fun-bafk'd fcenes I ftray,
As the fair landfcape leads my thoughtful way,
As upland path, oft winding, bids me rove
Where orange bowers invite, or olive grove,
No fullen phantoms brooding o'er my breaft,
The genial influence of the clime I tafte;
Yet ftill regardful of my native fhore,
In every fcene, my roaming eyes explore,
Whate'er its afpect, ftill, by memory brought,
My fading country rufhes on my thought.

While now perhaps the claffic page you turn,
And warm'd with honeft indignation burn,
'Till hopelefs, ficklied by the climate's gloom,
Your generous fears call forth Britannia's doom,
What hoftile fpears her facred lawns invade,
By friends deferted, by her chiefs betray'd,
Low fall'n and vanquifh'd!—I, with mind ferene
As Lifboa's fky, yet penfive as the fcene
Around, and penfive feems the fcene to me,
From other ills my country's fate forefee.

Not

[3]

Not from the hands that wield Iberia's fpear,

Not from the hands that Gaul's proud thunders bear,

Nor thofe that turn on Albion's breaft the fword

Beat down of late by Albion when it gored

Their own, who impious doom their parent's fall

Beneath the world's great foe th' infidious Gaul;

Yes, not from thefe the immedicable wound

Of Albion — Other is the bane profound

Deftined alone to touch her mortal part.;

Herfelf is fick and poifoned at the heart.

O'er Tago's banks where'er I roll mine eyes

The gallant deeds of antient days arife;

The fcenes the Lufian Mufes fond difplay'd

Before me oft, as oft at eve I ftray'd

By Ifis' hallowed ftream. Oft now the ftrand

Where Gama march'd his death-devoted * band,

ª The expedition of Vafco de Gama, the difcoverer of the Eaft-Indies, was extremely unpopular, as it was efteemed impracticable. His embarkation is ftrongly marked by Oforius the hiftorian. Gama, before he went on board, fpent the night along with the crews of his fquadron in the chapel of our Lady at Belem, on the fpot where the noble gothic church now ftands adjoining the convent of St. Jerome.

In the chapel they bound themfelves to obedience to Gama, and devoted themfelves

While

While Lifboa awed with horror faw him fpread

The daring fails that firft to India led;

And oft Almada's caftled fteep infpires

The penfive Mufe's vifionary fires;

Almada Hill to Englifh Memory dear,

While fhades of Englifh heroes wander here!

To ancient Englifh valour facred ftill

Remains, and ever fhall, Almada Hill;

The hill and lawns to Englifh valour given

What time the Arab Moons from Spain were driven,

Before the banners of the Crofs fubdued,

When Lifboa's towers were bathed in Moorifh blood

By Glofter's lance.—Romantic days that yield

Of gallant deeds a wide luxuriant field

Dear to the Mufe that loves the fairy plains

Where ancient honour wild and ardent reigns.

to death. " On the next day when the ad-
" venturers marched to the fhips, the fhore
" of Belem prefented one of the moft fo-
" lemn and affecting fcenes perhaps re-
" corded in hiftory. The beach was cover-
" ed with the inhabitants of Lifbon. A
" numerous proceffion of priefts in their
" robes fung anthems, and offered up invo-
" cations to heaven. Every one beheld the
" adventurers as brave innocent men going
" to a dreadful execution, as rufhing upon
" certain death." *Introduct. to the Lufiad.*

Where

Where high o'er Tago's flood Almada lowers,
Amid the folemn pomp of mouldering towers
Supinely feated, wide and far around
My eye delighted wanders. — Here the bound
Of fair Europa o'er the Ocean rears
Its weftern edge; where dimly difappears
The Atlantic wave, the flow defcending day
Mild beaming pours ferene the gentle ray
Of Lufitania's winter, filvering o'er
The tower-like fummits of the mountain fhore;
Dappling the lofty cliffs that coldly throw
Their fable horrors o'er the vales below.
Far round the ftately-fhoulder'd river bends
Its giant arms, and fea-like wide extends
Its midland bays, with fertile iflands crown'd,
And lawns for Englifh valour ftill renown'd:
Given to Cornwallia's gallant fons of yore,
Cornwallia's name the fmiling paftures bore;
And ftill their Lord his Englifh lineage boafts
From Rolland famous in the Croifade Hofts.

Where

Where fea-ward narrower rolls the fhining tide
Through hills by hills embofom'd on each fide,
Monaftic walls in every glen arife
In coldeft white fair gliftening to the fkies
Amid the brown-brow'd rocks; and, far as fight,
Proud domes and villages array'd in white[b]
Climb o'er the fteeps, and thro' the dufky green
Of olive groves, and orange bowers between,
Speckled with glowing red, unnumber'd gleam—
And Lifboa towering o'er the lordly ftream
Her marble palaces and temples fpreads
Wildly magnific o'er the loaded heads
Of bending hills, along whofe high-piled bafe
The port capacious, in a moon'd embrace,
Throws her maft-foreft, waving on the gale
The vanes of every fhore that hoifts the fail.

Here while the Sun from Europe's breaft retires,
Let Fancy, roaming as the fcene infpires,

[b] The houfes in Portugal are generally efteemed as repulfive of the rays of the
whitened on the outfide, white being Sun.

Purfue

Perfue the prefent and the paft reftore,

And Nature's purpofe in her fteps explore.

   Nor you, my Friend, admiring Rome, difdain

Th' Iberian fields and Lufitanian Spain.

While Italy, obfcured in tawdry blaze,

A motley, modern character difplays,

And languid trims her long exhaufted ftore;

Iberia's fields with rich and genuine ore

Of ancient manners wooe the traveller's eye;

And fcenes untraced in every landfcape lie.

Here every various dale with leffons fraught

Calls to the wanderer's vifionary thought

What mighty deeds the lofty hills of Spain

Of old have witnefs'd—From the evening main

Her mountain tops the Tyrian pilots faw

In lightnings wrapt, and thrill'd with facred awe

Thro' Greece the tales of Gorgons, Hydras fpread,

And Geryon dreadful with the triple head;

The

The ſtream of 'Lethe, and the dread abodes

Of forms gigantic, and infernal gods.

But ſoon, by fearlſs luſt of gold impell'd,

They mined the mountain, and explored the field ;

'Till Rome and Carthage, fierce for empire, ſtrove,

As for their prey two famiſh'd birds of Jove.

The rapid Durius then and Bœtis' flood

Were dyed with Roman and with Punic blood,

While oft the lengthening plains and mountain ſides

Seem'd moving on, flow rolling tides on tides,

When from Pyrene's ſummits Afric pour'd

Her armies, and o'er Rome deſtruction lour'd.

Here while the Youth revolves ſome Hero's fame,

If patriot zeal his Britiſh breaſt inflame,

Here let him trace the fields to freedom dear

Where low in duſt lay Rome's invading ſpear ;

* The river of Lima, in the north of Portugal, ſaid to be the Lethe of the ancients, is thus mentioned by Cellarius in his *Geographia Antiqua*; " Fabuloſus Oblivionis fluvius, Limæas, ultra Luſitaniam in ſeptentrione." It runs through a moſt romantic and beautiful diſtrict ; from which circumſtance it probably received the name of the River of Oblivion, the firſt ſtrangers who viſited it, forgetting their native country, and being willing to continue on its banks. The ſame reaſon of forgetfulneſs is aſcribed to the Lotos by Homer, O.lyſ. ix. There is another Lethe of the ancients in Africa.

Where

Where Viriatus * proudly trampled o'er
Fasces and Roman eagles steept in gore;
Or where he fell, with honest laurels crown'd,
The awful victim of a treacherous wound;
A wound still bathed in Honour's generous tear,
While Freedom's wounds the brave and good revere;
Still pouring fresh th' inexpiable stain
O'er Rome's patrician honour false and vain!

Or should the pride of bold revolt inspire,
And touch his bosom with unhallowed fire;
If merit spurn'd demand stern sacrifice,
O'er Ev'ra's * fields let dread Sertorius rise.
Dyed in his country's blood, in all the pride
Of wrongs revenged, illustrious let him ride
Enshrined, o'er Spain, in Victory's dazzling rays,
'Till Rome look pale beneath the mounting blaze.
But let the British wanderer thro' the dales
Of Ev'ra stray, while midnight tempest wails:

* This great man is called by Florus the Romulus of Spain. What is here said of him is agreeable to history.

* Ebora, now Evora, was the principal residence of Sertorius.

C

There

There as the hoary villagers relate
Sertorius, Sylla, Marius, weep their fate,
Their fpectres gliding on the lightning blue,
Oft doom'd their ancient ftations to renew;
Sertorius bleeding on Perpenna's knife,
And Marius finking in ambition's ftrife;
As foreft boars entangled in a chain,
Dragg'd on, as ftings each Leader's rage or pain;
And each the furious Leader in his turn,
'Till low they lie, a ghaftly wreck forlorn.

And fay, ye tramplers on your country's mounds,
Say who fhall fix the fwelling torrent's bounds?
Or who fhall fail the pilot of the flood?
Alas, full oft fome worthlefs trunk of wood
Is whirl'd into the port, blind Fortune's boaft,
While nobleft veffels, founder'd, ftrew the coaft!

If wars of fairer fame and old applaufe,
That bear the title of our country's caufe,

To

To humanife barbarians, and to raife
Our country's prowefs, their aflerted praife;
If thefe delight, Hifpania's dales difplay
The various arts and toils of Roman fway.
Here jealous Cato[f] laid the cities wafte,
And Julius[f] here in fairer pride replaced,
'Till ages faw the labours of the plough
By every river, and the barren bough
Of laurel fhaded by the olive's bloom,
And grateful Spain the ftrength of lordly Rome;
Hers mighty bards[g], and hers the facred earth
That gave the world a friend in Trajan's birth.

When Rome's wide empire, a luxurious prey,
Debafed in falfe refinement nervelefs lay,
The northern hords on Europe's various climes
Planted their ruling virtues and their crimes.
Cloifter'd by Tyber's ftream the flothful ftaid,
To Seine and Loire the gay and friv'lous ftray'd,

[f] According to Hiftory, this different policy is ftrikingly charactcriftic of thofe celebrated names.   [g] Lucan, Martial, Seneca.

C 2

A fordid

A fordid groupe the Belgian marfhes pleafed,
And Saxony's wild forefts Freedom feized,
There held her juries, poifed the legal fcales; —
And Spain's romantic hills and lonely dales
The penfive Lover fought; and Spain became
The land of gallantry and amorous flame.
Hail, favour'd clime! whofe lone retreats infpire
The fofteft dreams of languifhing defire,
Affections trembling with a glow all holy,
Wildly fublime, and fweetly melancholy;
'Till rapt devotion to the Fair, refine
And bend each paffion low at Honour's fhrine.
So felt the iron Goth when here he brought
His worfhip of the Fair with valour fraught:
Soon as Iberia's mountains fixt his home,
He rofe a character unknown to Rome;
His manners wildly colour'd as the flowers
And flaunting plumage of Brazilian bowers:
New to the world as thefe, yet polifh'd more
Than e'er the pupil of the Attic lore

Might

Might proudly boaſt. On man's bold arm robuſt
The tender Fair reclines with fondeſt truſt:
With Nature's fineſt touch exulting glows
The manly breaſt which that fond aid beſtows:
That firſt of generous joys on man beſtow'd,
In Gothic Spain in all its fervour glow'd.
Then high burn'd honour; and the dread alarms
Of danger then aſſumed the deareſt charms.
What for the Fair was dared or ſuffered, bore
A ſaint-like merit, and was envied more;
'Till led by love-ſick Fancy's dazzled flight,
From Court to Court forth roam'd Adventure's Knight;
And tilts and tournaments, in mimic wars,
Supplied the triumphs and the honour'd ſcars
Of arduous battles for their country fought,
'Till the keen reliſh of the marvellous wrought
All wild and fever'd; and each peaceful ſhade,
With batter'd armour deckt, its Knight diſplay'd,
In ſoothing tranſport, liſtening to the ſtrain
Of dwarfs and giants, and of monſters ſlain;

Of

Of fpells all horror, and enchanters dire,
And the fweet banquet of the amorous fire,
When Knights and Ladies chafte, · relieved from thrall,
Hold Love's high holiday in bower and hall.

'Twas thus, all pleafing to the languid thought,
With magic power the tales of magic wrought;
Till by the Mufes armed, in all the ire
Of wit, refiftlefs as electric fire,
Forth rode La Mancha's Knight; and fudden fled
Goblins and beauteous nymphs, and pagans dread,
As the delirious dream of ficknefs flies,
When health returning fmiles from vernal fkies.

But turn we now from Chivalry difeafed,
To Chivalry when Honour's wreath fhe feized
From Wifdom's hand. — From Taurus' rugged fteep,
And Caucafus, far round with headlong fweep,
As wolves wild howling from their famifh'd den,
Rufh'd the devouring bands of Sarazen:

Their

Their favage genius, giant-like and blind,

Trampling with fullen joy on human kind,

Affyria lay its own uncover'd grave,

And Gallia trembled to th' Atlantic wave :

In awful wafte the faireft cities moan'd,

And human Liberty expiring groan'd

When Chivalry arofe:—Her ardent eye

Sublime, that fondly mingled with the fky,

Where patience watch'd, and ftedfaft purpofe frown'd

Mixt with Devotion's fire, fhe darted round,

Stern and indignant; on her glittering fhield

The Crofs fhe bore, and proudly to the field

High plumed fhe rufh'd; by Honour's dazzling fired,

Confcious of Heaven's own caufe, and all infpired

By holy vows, as on the frowning tower

The lightning vollies, on the crefted power

Of Sarazen fhe wing'd her javelin's way,

And the wide-wafting giant proftrate lay.

Let

Let fupercilious Wifdom's fmiling pride
The paffion wild of thefe bold days deride;
But let the humbler Sage with reverence own
That fomething facred glows, of name unknown, }
Glows in the deeds that Heaven delights to crown;
Something that boafts an impulfe uncontroul'd
By fchool-taught prudence, and its maxims cold.
Fired at the thought, methinks on facred ground
I tread; where'er I caft mine eyes around,
Palmela's hill* and Cintra's fummits tell
How the grim Sarazen's dread legions fell;
Turbans and cymeters in carnage roll'd,
And their moon'd enfigns torn from every hold : —
Yes, let the Youth whofe generous fearch explores
The various leffons of Iberia's fhores,
Let him as wandering at the Mufe's hour
Of eve or morn where low the Moorifh tower,
Fallen from its rocky height and tyrant fway,
Lies fcatter'd o'er the dale in fragments grey,

* Palmela's hill and Cintra's fummits —
are both feen from Almada, and were principal forts of the Moors. They were
ftormed by Alphonfo the firft about the time
of the conqueft of Lifbon.

Let

Let him with joy behold the hills around

With olive forefts, and with vineyards crown'd,

All grateful pouring on the hands that rear

Their fruit, the fruitage of the bounteous year.

Then let his mind to fair Ionia turn, —

Alas! how wafte Ionia's landfcapes mourn;

And thine, O beauteous Greece, amid the towers

Where dreadful ftill the Turkifh banner lowers;

Beneath whofe gloom, unconfcious of the ftain

That dims his foul, the peafant hugs his chain.

And whence thefe woes debafing human kind?

Eunuchs in heart, in polifh'd floth reclin'd,

Thy fons, degenerate Greece, ignobly bled,

And fair Byzantium bow'd th' imperial head;

While Tago's iron race, in dangers fteel'd,

All ardour, dared the horrors of the field.

The towers of Venice trembled o'er her flood,

And Paris' gates aghaft and open ftood;

Low

Low lay her Peers on Fontarabia's [i] plains :

And Lifboa groan'd beneath ftern Mah'met's chains :

Vain was the hope the North might reft unfpoil'd ;

When ftern Iberia's fpirit fierce recoil'd.

As from the toils the wounded lion bounds,

And tears the hunters and the fated hounds ;

So fmarting with his wounds th' Iberian tore,

And to his fun-fcorch'd regions drove, the Moor :

The vengeful Moors, as maftiffs on their prey,

Return'd ; as heavy clouds their deep array

Blacken'd o'er Tago's banks. — As Sagrez [k] braves

And ftems the furious rage of Afric's waves,

So braved, fo ftood the Lufitanian bands,

The fouthern bulwark of Europa's lands.

[i] The irruption of the Mohammedans into Europe gave rife to that fpecies of poetry called Romance. The Orlando Furiofo is founded upon the invafion of France,

> When Charlemaigne with all his Peerage fell
> By Fontarabia ——   MILTON.

[k] The promontory of Sagrez, where Henry, Duke of Vifeo, refided and eftablifhed his naval fchool, is on the fouthern part of Portugal oppofite to Africa.

Such

Such were the foes by Chivalry repell'd,
And such the honours that adorn'd her shield.
And ask what Christian Europe owes the high
And ardent soul of gallant Chivalry,
Ask, and let Turkish Europe's groans reply !

As through the pictured abbey window gleams
The evening Sun with bold though fading beams,
So through the reverend shade of ancient days
Gleam these bold deeds with dim yet golden rays.
But let not glowing Fancy as it warms
O'er these, high honour's youthful pride in arms,
Forget the stern ambition and the worth
Of minds mature, by patriot Kings call'd forth;
That worth that roused the nations to explore
Old Ocean's wildest waves and farthest shore.

By human eye untempted, unexplored,
An awful solitude, old Ocean roar'd :

As

As to the fearful dove's impatient eye
Appears the height untry'd of upper fky;
So feem'd the laft dim wave, in boundlefs fpace
Involved and loft, when Tago's gallant race,
As eagles fixing on the Sun their eyes
Through gulphs unknown explor'd the morning fkies;
And taught the wondering world the grand defign
Of parent heaven, that fhore to fhore fhould join
In bands of mutual aid, from fky to fky,
And Ocean's wildeft waves the chain fupply.

And here, my Friend, how many a trophy wooes
The Briton's earneft eye, and Britifh Mufe!
Here bids the youthful Traveller's care forego
The arts of elegance and polifh'd fhew;
Bids other arts his nobler thoughts engage,
And wake to higheft aim his patriot rage;
Thofe arts which raifed that race of Men, who fhone
The heroes of their age on Lifboa's throne.

What

What mighty deeds in filial order flow'd,

While each ftill brighter than its parent glow'd,

Till Henry's Naval School its heroes pour'd

From pole to pole wherever Ocean roar'd !

Columbus, Gama, and Magellan's name,

Its deathlefs boaft; and all of later fame

Its offspring—kindling o'er the view the Mufe

The naval pride of thofe bright days reviews;

Sees Gama's fails, that firft to India bore,

In awful hope evanifh from the fhore;

Sees from the filken regions of the morn

What fleets of gay triumphant vanes return !

What heroes, plumed with conqueft, proudly bring

The Eaftern fceptres to the Lufian King !

When fudden, rifing on the evening gale,

Methinks I hear the Ocean's murmurs wail,

And every breeze repeat the woeful tale,

How bow'd, how fell proud Lifboa's naval throne—

Ah heaven, how cold the boding thoughts rufh on !

Methinks

Methinks I hear the fhades that hover round
Of Englifh heroes heave the figh profound,
Prophetic of the kindred fate that lowers,
O'er Albion's fleets and London's proudeft towers.

Broad was the firm-bafed ftructure and fublime,
That Gama fondly rear'd on India's clime:
On juftice and benevolence he placed
Its ponderous weight, and warlike trophies graced
Its mounting turrets; and o'er Afia wide
Great Albuquerk[1] renown'd its generous pride.
The injured native fought its friendly fhade,
And India's Princes bleft its powerful aid:
Till from corrupted paffion's bafeft hour
Rofe the dread dæmon of tyrannic power.
Sámpayo's heart, where dauntlefs valour reign'd,
And counfel deep, fhe feiz'd and foul profaned.

---

[1] Albuquerk, Sampayo, Nunio, Caftro, are diftinguifhed characters in the Lufiad, and in the Hiftory of Portuguefe Afia.

Then

Then the ftraight road where facred juftice leads,

Where for its plighted compact honour bleeds,

Was left, and holy patriot zeal gave place

To luft of gold and felf-devotion bafe:

Deceitful art the Chief's fole guide became,

And breach of faith was wifdom; flaughter, fame.

Yet though from far his hawk-eye markt its prey,

Soon through the rocks that croft his crooked way,

As a toil'd bull, fiercely he ftumbled on,

Till low he lay difhonour'd and o'erthrown.

Others, without his valour or his art,

With all his interefted rage of heart,

Follow'd, as blighting mifts on Gama's toil,

And undermined and rent the mighty pile;

Convulfions dread its deep foundations tore,

Its bending head the fcath of lightning bore:

Its falling turrets defolation fpread;

And from its faithlefs fhade in horror fled

The

The native tribes—yet not at once fubdued;

Its priftine ftrength long ftorms on ftorms withftood :

A Nunio's juftice, and a Caftro's fword,

Oft raifed its turrets, and its dread reftored.

Yet, like the funfhine of a winter day

On Norway's coaft, foon died the tranfient ray.

A tyrant race, who own'd no country *, came,

Deep to intrench themfelves their only aim ;

With luft of rapine fever'd and athirft,

With the unhallowed rage of game accurft ;

Againft each fpring of action, on the breaft

For wifeft ends, by Nature's hand impreft,

Stern war they waged ; and blindly ween'd, alone

On brutal dread, to fix their cruel throne.

The wife and good, with indignation fired,

Silent from their unhallowed board retired ;

ᵐ *A tyrant race, who own'd no country, came,* — before the total declenfion of the Portuguefe in Afia ; and while they were fubject to Spain, the principal people, fays the hiftorian Faria, who were moftly a mixed race born in India, loft all affection for the mother country, nor had any regard for any of the provinces where they were only the fons of ftrangers : and prefent emolument became their fole object.

The

The Bafe and Cunning ftaid, and, flaves avow'd,
Submifs to every infult fmiling bow'd.
Yet while they fmiled and bow'd the abject head,
In chains unfelt their Tyrant Lords they led;
Their av'rice, watching as a bird of prey,
O'er every weaknefs, o'er each vice held fway;
Till fecret art affumed the thwarting face,
And dictate bold; and ruin and difgrace
Clofed the unworthy fcene. Now trampled low
Beneath the injured native, and the foe
From Belgia lured by India's coftly prey,
Thy glorious ftructure, Gama, proftrate lay;
And lies in defolated awful gloom,
Dread and inftructive as a ruin'd tomb.

Nor lefs on Tago's than on India's coaft
Was ancient Lufian Virtue ftain'd and loft:
On Tago's banks, heroic ardour's foes,
A foft, luxurious, tinfel'd race, arofe;

Of

Of lofty boaftful look and pompous fhew,
Triumphant tyrants o'er the weak and low :
Yet wildly ftarting from the gaming board
At every diftant brandifh of the fword ;
Already conquer'd by uncertain dread,
Imploring peace with feeble hands outfpread ; —
Such peace as trembling fuppliants ftill obtain,
Such peace they found beneath the yoke of Spain ;
And the wide empires of the Eaft no more
Poured their redundant horns on Lifboa's fhore.

Alas, my Friend, how vain the faireft boaft
Of human pride ! how foon is Empire loft !
The pile by ages rear'd to awe the world,
By one degenerate race to ruin hurl'd !
And fhall the Briton view that downward race
With eye unmoved, and no fad likenefs trace !
Ah heaven ! in every fcene, by memory brought,
My fading country rufhes on my thought.

From

From Lifboa now the frequent vefper bell
Vibrates o'er Tago's ftream with folemn knell.

Turn'd by the call my penfive eye furveys
That mighty fcene of Hift'ry's fhame and praife.

Methinks I hear the yells of horror rife
From flaughter'd thoufands fhricking ⁿ to the fkies,

As factious rage or blinded zeal of yore
Roll'd their dire chariot wheels through ftreams of gore.

Now throbs of other glow my foul employ;
I hear the triumph of a nation's joy °,

ⁿ Befides the total flaughter of the Moors at the taking of Lifbon, other maffacres have
bathed the ftreets of that city in blood. King Fernando, furnamed the Carelefs, was
driven from Lifbon by a bloody infurrection, headed by one Velafquez a Taylor. Some
time after on the death of Fernando, Andeyro, the Queen's favourite, was ftabbed in her
prefence, the Bifhop of Lifbon was thrown from the tower of his own cathedral, and the
maffacre of all the Queen's adherents became general; and many were murdered under that
pretence, by thofe who had an enmity againft them. In 1505 between two and three
thoufand Jews were maffacred in Lifbon in the fpace of three days, and many Chriftians
were alfo murdered by their private enemies under a fimilar pretence that they were of the
Hebrew race. Thoufands flocked in from the country to affift in their deftruction, and the
crews of fome French and Dutch fhips then in the river, fays Oforius, were particularly
active in murdering and plundering.

° When the Spanifh yoke was thrown off, and the Duke of Braganza afcended the
throne under the title of John IV. This is one of the moft remarkable events in hiftory,
and does the Portuguefe nation infinite honour.

E 2   From

From bondage refcued and the foreign fword,
And Independence and the Throne reftored !

Hark, what low found from Cintra rock ! the air
Trembles with horror ; fainting lightnings glare ;
Shrill crows the cock, the dogs give difmal yell ;
And with the whirlwind's roar full comes the fwell ;
Convulfive ftaggers rock th' eternal ground,
And heave the Tagus from his bed profound ;
A dark red cloud the towers of Lifboa veils ;
Ah heaven, what dreadful groan ! the rifing gales
Bring light ; and Lifboa fmoaking in the duft
Lies. fall'n. — The wide-fpread ruins, ftill auguft,
Still fhew the footfteps where the dreadful God
Of earthquake, cloath'd in howling darknefs, trod ;
Where mid foul weeds the heaps of marble tell
From what proud height the fpacious temples fell ;
And penury and floth of fqualid >mien
Beneath the rooflefs palace walls * are feen

⁕ This defcription is literally juft. Whole families, of all ages, are every where feen
among the ruins, the only covering of their habitations being ragged fragments of fail-

In

[29]

In favage hovels, where the tap'ftried floor
Was trod by Nobles and by Kings before;
How like, alas, her Indian empire's ftate!
How like the city's and the nation's fate!
Yet Time points forward to a brighter day;
Points to the domes that ftretch their fair array
Through the brown ruins, lifting to the fky
A loftier brow and mien of promife high;
Points to the river-fhore where wide and grand
The Courts of Commerce and her walks expand,
As an Imperial palace⁹ to retain
The Univerfal Queen, and fix her reign;
Where pleas'd fhe hears the groaning oar refound;
By magazines and ars'nals mounded round,

---

cloth; and their common bed dirty ftraw. The magnificent and extenfive ruins of the
palace of Braganza contain feveral hundreds of thefe idle people, much more wretched
in their appearance than the gypfies of England.

⁹ The *Praça de Commercio*, or Forum of Commerce, is one of the largeft and moft
magnificent fquares in Europe. Three fides confift of the Exchange and the public
offices; the fourth is formed by the Tagus, which is here edged by an extenfive and
noble wharf, built of coarfe marble.

Whofe

Whofe yet unfinifhed grandeur proudly boafts
The faireft hope of either India's coafts,
And bids the Mufe's eye in vifion roam
Through mighty fcenes in ages long to come.

Forgive, fair Thames, the fong of truth that pays
To Tago's emprefs-ftream fuperior praife;
O'er every vauntful river be it thine
To boaft the guardian fhield of laws divine;
But yield to Tagus all the fovereign ftate
By Nature's gift beftow'd and partial Fate,
The fea-like port and central fway to pour
Her fleets, by happieft courfe, on every fhore.

When from the fleep of ages dark and dead,
Thy Genius, Commerce, rear'd her infant head,
Her cradle bland on Tago's lap fhe chofe,
And foon to wandering childhood fprightly rofe;
And when to green and youthful vigour grown
On Tago's breaft fhe fixt her central throne;

Far

Far from the hurricane's refiftlefs fweep
That tears with thundering rage the Carib deep;
Far from the foul-winged Winter that deforms
And rolls the northern main with ftorms on ftorms;
Beneath falubrious fkies, to fummer gales
She gives the ventrous and returning fails:
The fmiling ifles, named Fortunate of old,
Firft on her Ocean's bofom fair unfold:
Thy world, Columbus, fpreads its various breaft,
Proud to be firft by Lifboa's waves careft;
And Afric wooes and leads her eafy way
To the fair regions of the rifing day.
If Turkey's drugs invite or filken pride,
Thy ftraits, Alcides, give the ready tide;
And turn the prow, and foon each fhore expands
From Gallia's coaft to Europe's northern lands.

When Heaven decreed low to the duft to bring
That lofty oak', Affyria's boaftful King,

¹ See Daniel, ch. iv.

Deep,

Deep, faid the angel voice, the roots fecure
With bands of brafs, and let the life endure,
For yet his head fhall rife.—And deep remain
The living roots of Lifboa's ancient reign,
Deep in the caftled ifles on Afia's ftrand,
And firm in fair Brazilia's wealthy land.
And fay, while ages roll their length'ning train,
Shall Nature's gifts to Tagus ftill prove vain,
An idle wafte !—A dawn of brighteft ray
Has boldly promifed the returning day
Of Lifboa's honours, fairer than her prime
Loft by a rude unletter'd Age's crime—
Now Heaven-taught Science and her liberal band
Of Arts, and dictates by experience plann'd,
Beneath the fmiles of a benignant Queen
Boaft the fair opening of a reign ' ferene,

' Alludes to the eftablifhment of the Royal Academy of Lifbon in July 1780, under
the prefidency of the moft illuftrious Prince Don John of Braganza, Duke of Lafoens,
&c. &c. &c. The Author was prefent at the ceremony of its commencement, and had
the honour to be admitted a member.

[33]

Of omen high.—And Camoens' Ghoſt no more

Wails the neglected Muſe on Tago's ſhore;

No more his tears the barbarous Age ' upbraid:

His griefs and wrongs all ſooth'd, his happy Shade

Beheld th' Ulyſſes ʷ of his age return

To Tago's banks; and earneſt to adorn

The Hero's brows, he weaves the Elyſian crown,

What time the letter'd Chiefs of old renown,

ᵗ Camoens, the firſt poet of Portugal, publiſhed his Luſiad at a time of the deepeſt declenſion of public virtue, when the Portugueſe empire in India was falling into rapid decay, when literature was totally neglected, and all was luxury and imbecility at home. At the end of books V. and VII. of his Luſiad, he ſeverely upbraids the Nobility for their barbarous ignorance. He died, neglected in a workhouſe, a few months before his country fell under the yoke of Philip II. of Spain, whoſe policy in Portugal was of the ſame kind with that which he exerciſed in the Netherlands, endeavouring to ſecure ſub-miſſion by ſeverity, with the view of reducing them beneath the poſſibility of a ſucceſs-ful revolt.

ʷ This title is given by the Portugueſe hiſtorians to Don John, one of the younger ſons of John I. of Portugal, who had viſited every Court of Europe. The ſame title is no leſs due to the preſent illuſtrious deſcendant of his family, the Duke of Lafoens. His Grace, who has within theſe few years returned to his native country, was about twenty-two years abſent from it. During the late War, he was a volunteer in the army of the Empreſs Queen, in which he ſerved as Lieutenant-general, and particularly diſtinguiſhed himſelf at the battle of Maxen, where the Pruſſians were defeated. After the peace, he not only viſited every court of Europe, moſt of whoſe languages he ſpeaks fluently, but alſo travelled to Turkey and Egypt, and even to Lapland. His Grace is no leſs diſtinguiſhed by his taſte for the *Belles Lettres*, than for his extenſive knowledge of Hiſtory and Science.

F　　　　　　And

And patriot Heroes, in the Elyſian bowers
Shall hail Braganza: of the faireſt flowers
Of Helicon, entwined with laurel leaves
From Maxen field, the deathleſs wreath he weaves ;
Anxious alone, nor be his vows in vain !
That long his toil unfiniſhed may remain !

  The view how grateful to the liberal mind,
Whoſe glow of heart embraces human kind,
To ſee a nation riſe ! But ah, my Friend,
How dire the pangs to mark our own deſcend !
With ample powers from ruin ſtill to ſave,
Yet as a veſſel on the furious wave,
Through ſunken rocks and rav'nous whirlpools toſt,
Each power to ſave in counter-action loſt,
Where, while combining ſtorms the decks o'erwhelm,
Timidity ſlow faulters at the helm,
The crew, in mutiny, from every maſt
Tearing its ſtrength, and yielding to the blaſt ;

By

By Faction's ſtern and gloomy luſt of change,
And ſelfiſh rage inſpired and dark revenge —
Nor ween, my Friend, that favouring Fate forebodes
That Albion's ſtate, the toil of demi-gods,
From ancient manners pure, through ages long,
And from unnumber'd friendly aſpects ſprung;
When poiſon'd at the heart its foul expires,
Shall e'er again relume its generous fires :
No future day may ſuch fair Frame reſtore :
When Albion falls, ſhe falls to riſe no more.